# The Adventures of ARNIE the DOUGHNUT

### The SPINNY ICKY SHOWDOWN

written and illustrated by
## LAURIE KELLER

SCHOLASTIC INC.

For my most favorite Otie-kins:
Elena, Vincent, and Francis

Thank you to my clever friends and family for their "ICK games"
inspiration and feedback: JoAnn Adinolfi, Brendan Callahan, Evan Callahan,
Meg Cundiff, Galen Fott, Sarah Halliday, Charise Mericle Harper,
Rob Hatem, Rilynne Locke, Scott Mack, Charlie McCarthy, Kerry Meyer,
Carol Osborne, Christy Ottaviano, Deb Pilutti, Marilyn Quail,
Jenny Whitehead, Pete Whitehead, and Amy Young.

ISBN 978-1-338-03219-2

12 11 10 9 8 7 6 5 4 3 2 1                    16 17 18 19 20 21

Printed in the U.S.A.                                    40

First Scholastic printing, March 2016

The illustrations for this book were created by using black felt-tip pens and Photoshop.

# CHAPTER 1

They're crossed!

What about yours, Peezo?

Fingers, toes, and eyes!

Mine too!

4

DARN, I would have liked a fancy new thing-amajig, but we CAN'T uncross our fingers because RICKy MaverICK, the host of *The SPINNY ICKy SHOWDOWN*, is about to announce the **one** and **only** town they're going to travel to for their season finale! *The SPINNY ICKy SHOWDOWN* is the BEST show on TV, and Peezo and I want to compete on it more than anything. Even Mr. Bing likes to watch it, which is saying a lot because he doesn't like the shows

# DING DONG DOOFUS,

# NOGGIN KNOCKERS,

## OR

# PLEASE STOP SNEEZING ON ME!

Peezo comes over every Friday night to watch *The SPINNY ICKy SHOWDOWN* with us. We laugh really hard through the whole show because the *ICKSTERS* (the contestants) have to do all sorts of crazy

# iCK-related things

like painting a piCKet fence with lipstiCK or jumping like criCKets over candlestiCKs.

The *ICKSTERS* compete in teams of two and one team gets eliminated after each round. At the end of the competition both members of the winning *ICKS* team are presented with a **BIG, SHINY ICKS TROPHY** with their **VERY OWN NAME** engraved on it!

*The SPINNY ICKY SHOWDOWN CHAMPION*

YOUR NAME HERE

When Peezo and I heard that *The SPINNY ICKy SHOWDOWN* was taking their show on the road, we sent in our entry forms *RIGHT AWAY* hoping they'd pick *YUMMY VALLEY* and choose us to be an *ICKSTER* team! We had to make up a team name so we chose

# The DOUGH BROS

since we're both made of dough and we're **SUCH GOOD FRIENDS** we're almost like brothers, or **BROS** for short.

7

We're back, everyone, and it's the moment you've all been waiting for. We're ready to announce the one and only town we'll visit for the season finale of *The SPINNY ICKY SHOWDOWN*! DRUM ROLL, PLEASE.
Eh-hem, I said, ***DRUM ROLL PLEASE!***
That's ODD. Drum Roll Guy is ALWAYS right here whenever I call for a drum roll.
Does anyone know where he is?

10

# CHAPTER 2

YAY! YAY!
YAY!

He said YUMMY VALLEY, Peezo! He said YUMMY VALLEY!

13

Awww, no **WONDER** it's called *CRUMMY* Valley—nothing good *EVER* happens here!

That's not true! I'll be performing my popular *BURP* and *BELCH* show tonight at the *Dirtball Theater* in *Crummy Valley*. I'll be **DEBUTING** seven new bur—r—r—r—r—ps!

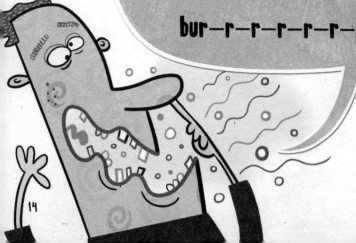

14

Pardonnez-moi for interrupting but **DEBUT** is a French word and is pronounced day-BYOO — not dee-BUTT as you may have thought. It means "first public appearance or performance."

All right, everyone in *Yummy Valley*, listen up. Here are the names of the five teams of *ICKSTERS* who will get their chance to take on *The SPINNY ICKY SHOWDOWN!*

**The Law Lads**
Officers Pete Pamby and Dwayne Dwaggy

**The Woolly Warriors**
Carl Caveman and Baa-Baa

**The Curly-Cues**
Identical Twins Heeza and Leeza Schmelly

**The Grand Gals**
Grandma Gloria and Granddaughter Gabby

# AND

Oh, please say the *Dough Bros*, PLEASE SAY THE *DOUGH BROS*!

Okay, I'll say it— the *Dough Bros*, Arnie the Doughnut and Peezo the Piece of Pizza!

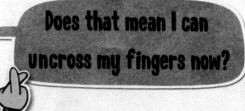

# LEAPIN' LONG JOHNS!

I can't believe that Peezo and I are actually going to **COMPETE** on *The SPINNY ICKy SHOWDOWN* and have a chance to win a big, shiny *ICKS* trophy! It sure would look nice up on Mr. Bing's shelf. Besides, I think Stiffy Stu McShiny up there would really like to have a buddy. Stiffy Stu McShiny is Mr. Bing's 1st place bowling trophy.

What do you say, Stiffy Stu—would you like to have a shiny new friend? You'll have to make some room up on that shelf because the *ICKS* trophy is even bigger than **YOU!**

# CHAPTER 3

Peezo and I have to get down to business, as they say, if we're going to stand a chance of winning The *SPINNY ICKy SHOWDOWN!* We need to get as fast, limber, and strong as possible to be ready for whatever they make us do. But there's ANOTHER reason we need to get stronger—a LOT stronger— and it involves the one thing that Peezo is

## MOST AFRAID OF IN THE WHOLE WIDE WORLD.....

Nick Pumpernickel is a pumped-up loaf of pumpernickel bread and the most DREADED category on *The SPINNY ICKy SHOWDOWN!* He's the former *MR. WORLD WONDER LOAF* and calls himself the *PUMPERNATOR!*

HA! The *PUMPERNATOR'S* muscles are too pumped up to fit on one page!

Of all the categories on the wheel, Nick Pumpernickel is the one NOBODY wants to get because each *ICKSTER* team has to ARM WRESTLE HIM!

Nick Pumpernickel is **SO STRONG** that he even takes on both teammates at the same time—

one with his **RIGHT** arm

and one with his **LEFT**.

He taunts everyone by acting all **TOUGH** and saying rude things before they start, and it must work because **NO ONE** has **EVER** beaten him. If they **DID**, they'd get to jump all the way ahead to the final round. But since that's

**NEVER** happened, the way it works is, the team who lasts the **SHORTEST** amount of time against Nick Pumpernickel gets

# DISQUALIFIED!
# ELIMINATED!
# KICKED OFF!

The teams who get to stay, though, are usually **SO TIRED** after arm wrestling him that it makes the rest of the competition even **HARDER** for them. The whole round is

# TOTALLY
# HUMILIATING

for everyone. Well, for everyone except **NICK PUMPERNICKEL**, that is!

I don't care what anyone thinks—I'm not afraid of the *PUMPERNATOR*, and Peezo shouldn't be either. I know this sounds CUCKOO, but I really think we can BEAT Nick Pumpernickel if we start training right away!

Did someone say *BEATNIK*?

Oh, hi, Beatnik Bill. No, I said BEAT NICK. As in, I think Peezo and I can BEAT Nick Pumpernickel at arm wrestling.

Yeah, right. Well, good luck with THAT! Later, little doughy-dude!

I get the feeling he doesn't agree with me.

# CHAPTER 4

There's a gym here at the apartment complex with lots of heavy weights to lift so we can get pumped up like that over-cooked bread-head, Nick Pumpernickel!

Come on, Peezo, it's time to pump some iron!

Okay, Peezo and I are all warmed up and ready to tone our **BUNS OF DOUGH!** We just heard the trainer lady tell that man to lift those barbells over his head **TEN** times. It must be working because even his **MUSCLES** have **MUSCLES!**

Three more!

All right, Peezo—you heard the lady. Let's lift these barbells over our heads ten times.

Maybe we should try lifting just ONE of them.

TOGETHER.

33

# CHAPTER 5

ICK! ICK! ICK! ICK! ICK! ICK!

Almost the **ENTIRE** town of *YUMMY VALLEY* is here waiting for *The SPINNY ICKy SHOWDOWN* bus to arrive!

Everyone is BUZZING about how surprising it is that the show is allowed to take place in this field. I mean, it's a perfectly fine field—even though it's loaded with HUGE CLUMPS of **BUMPS, HUMPS,** and **LUMPS** like most of our roads in *YUMMY VALLEY*. It's just that it happens to be right next door to the home of Maude Ellen Murky—better known as the

**GRUMP on a STUMP!**

She got her nickname because anytime anyone gets even CLOSE to her yard she climbs up on the big stump next to her house and yells,

GET OFF MY LAWN!

But apparently she's a big fan of the show and doesn't mind having the competition take place so close to her house. Well, hopefully that's true and she won't

## BITE ANYONE'S

## HEAD OFF TODAY!

I'm **RICKY MAVERICK**, the SPINNY, **ICK**Y host of *The SPINNY ICKY SHOWDOWN*! Please pardon my wrinkled suit, folks, but it was a **ROUGH RIDE** due to all the bumps, humps, and lumps on your roads! Our bus took QUITE a beating and two of my hairs actually popped out of place!

ANYWAY, before we meet the *YUM*—I mean, *LUMPY—VALLEY ICKSTERS*, let's take a peek at what they're all competing for—the big, shiny, *SPINNY ICKY SHOWDOWN* trophy!

The ★ SPINNY ICKY SHOWDOWN ★ CHAMPION

WOW!

Ooohh!

Ahh!

Ooohh!

YOUR NAME HERE

**HOLEY DOUGHNUTS**—it's even **BIGGER** and **SHINIER** than I imagined! I can't wait to see the look on Stiffy Stu's face when he lays his eyes on it!

# CHAPTER 6

All right, everyone—let's meet our *LUMPY VALLEY ICKSTERS*, shall we?

## The Curly-Cues
Heeza and
Leeza Schmelly

## The Woolly Warriors
Carl Caveman
and Baa-Baa

## The Grand Gals
Grandma Gloria and
Granddaughter Gabby

You can call me BIG G!

You can call me LITTLE G!

WOW, Little G has the BEST HAT! It has a propeller-spinning penguin on top! Don't ask me why, but I've always had a fondness for propeller-spinning penguins.

Why do

AH! I told you not to ask me why.

I like your hat.

I like your SPRINKLES.

Next we have

**The LAW LADS**

Officers Pete Pamby

and Dwayne Dwaggy.

Sadly, Dwayne Dwaggy dwopped—

I mean, *DROPPED*—out at the

last minute because of

an unfortunate hangnail

incident. SO, just moments

ago a NEW teammate was chosen from

the entries we received and that person is:

Drum roll, please!

d-r-r-r-r-r-r-r-r

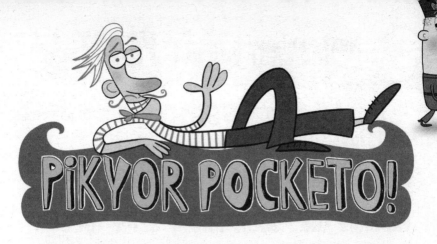

# PiKYOR POCKETO!

Mr. Pocketo recently moved here from the little island of *KLEPTONIA*. Since Pikyor Pocketo isn't a police officer or *LAW LAD* like Pete Pamby, they thought it best to change their team name. And since both of their FIRST and LAST names start with **P**s they decided on

## The *P. P. BOYS!*

Hmm, it doesn't sound as TOUGH when you say it out loud like that, does it?

And LAST but not *YEAST*—

Ba dum TSSSHH!

**HA,** a little baking joke there— we have the *DOUGH BROS*, Arnie the Doughnut and Peezo the Piece of Pizza.

I believe you boys are the first FOOD contestants we've had on the show.

So, do you think you'll RISE to the occasion?
And make TOAST of your opponents?
Will you COOK your competition?
Do you have the SKILLET takes?
STOP! IT'S TOO MUCH! I'M TAKING ANOTHER VACATION!

And two last introductions before we get started:

FIRST, the *ICKY CHICKEN*! When a round is about to begin, she'll **BAWK** three times like this:

bawk bawk baGAAWWK!

That's your cue to get moving!

And FINALLY, the ONE you've been waiting for—the DOUGHIEST of the DOUGHY, the DENSEST of the DENSE, the YEASTIEST of the YEASTY, the *"PUMPERNATOR"* himself— **NICK PUMPERNICKEL!**

That's right, it's the *Pumperlicious Pumpernator*! Nick Pumpern**ick**el knows you're shaking in your little baby socks, but the *Pumpernator's* not afraid of you wimpy *ICKSTER* sissies!

It's okay, Peezo, don't let him scare you. He talks **TOUGH** but he's all **FLUFF**!

Hello, Peezo, I see N**ick** Pumpern**ick**el has you *ALL SHOOK UP*, so my sideburns and I wrote you a little song. I hope it helps.

It's "The KING"!

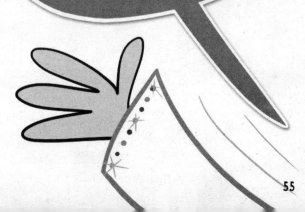

Thank you, thank you very much!

Say, are there any JELLY doughnuts around here? OOPS, never mind. GOOD LUCK, LITTLE DOUGH BROS!

# CHOPSTiCK NiCKEL PiCK!

In this round you have to find the NiCKELS we've hidden all over the large, lumpy bumps in the *Lumpy Valley* field.

That may sound **easy** but you won't be using your HANDS to pick them up. You'll be using a pair of SUPER DELUXE, EXTRA-LONG CHOPSTiCKs from *Elaine's Super Deluxe Extra-Long Chopstick Emporium!*

www.elainessuperdeluxeextralongchopstickemporium.com

OH—and you'll be wearing KN**ICK**ERS.

What are KN**ICK**ERS?

Well, there are **TWO** kinds. **ONE** is a kind of men's baggy-kneed trousers popular in the early 20th century worn in such sports as golf, baseball, and skiing to name a few. And the **OTHER** kind is, ummm . . . errrr . . . ladies' old-fashioned underpants.

Which kind will *WE* be wearing?

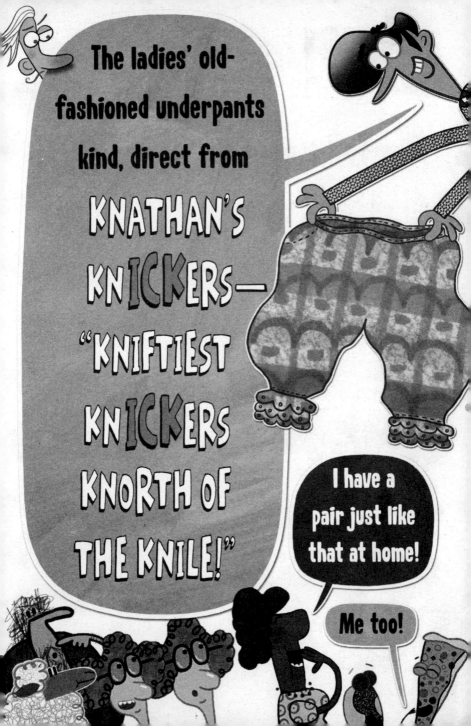

And here's the **KICKER**! Each team will **SHARE** a pair of **KNICKERS** (also known as ladies' old-fashioned underpants)—one *ICKSTER* in EACH leg! It might be **TRICKY** to run this way, but try and move **QUICKLY** because you only have three minutes to **PICK** the **NICKELS** and drop them in your **KNICKERS** (also known as ladies' old-fashioned underpants)!

The four teams with the most nickels will move to the next round, but the team with the least will have to leave with nothing but their few measly nickels and a single, unattractive pair of knickers (also known as ladies' old-fashioned underpants).

**COOL!** Peezo and I are **GREAT** at using chopsticks! Whenever Mr. Bing and his bowling pals order Chinese food, they let us play with their chopsticks after they finish eating. They're perfect for picking up and re-applying my sprinkles and Peezo's toppings after we get into one of our fake wrestling matches. But we've never used them while wearing ladies' old-fashioned underpants!

Also known as knickers!

All right, everyone, **TIME'S UP!** Please move to the judges' table and remove all the nickels from your knickers and drop them into the wicker baskets to be counted.

OH, NO! Our nickels are GONE!

Ours are gone too!

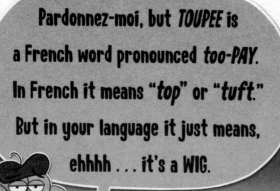

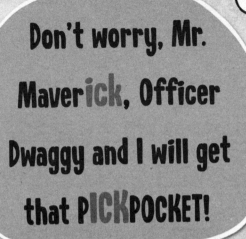

Don't worry, Mr. Maverick, Officer Dwaggy and I will get that PICKPOCKET!

But—my HANGNAIL!

Here, Mr. Maverick, I can give you a chocolate-frosting do until you get your wig back—err, I mean, *TOUPEE.*

Frosting do's are all the rage in Paris.

A few sprinkles on top would look nice.

**YES!** Ricky Maverick just told us that since the P. P. Boys are gone, no one has to be eliminated and **ALL** remaining *ICKSTERS* get to advance to ROUND TWO!

# WOOHOO!!!

# CHAPTER 8

I have to admit, I'm kind of relieved that Officer Pamby is gone. He always looks at me like he wants to buy me a **ONE-WAY** ticket to his stomach! At least now I can focus on the competition and have **FUN**. I sure wish Peezo could do the same. He's so worried about the possibility of having to face NICK PUMPERNICKEL that he's not acting like himself.

All right, ICKSTERS, get ready, the wheel is slowing down and it looks like it's going to stop on . . .
BLOOD-THIRSTY TICKS
Oooh, a NEW category!

It says here that in this round, members of a hungry giant **TICK** family will latch on to and suck the blood of each **ICKSTER** until—

# WHAT?

That's the most **DISGUSTING** thing I've ever heard! Who made up this category, anyway?

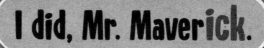

I did, Mr. Maverick.

Who are *YOU*?

Donald Tick, the new assistant category developer. It's my first day.

And your LAST too, I'm sorry to say. That's not the kind of thing we're looking for on *The SPINNY ICKY SHOWDOWN*!

# ATTENTION, EVERYONE!

The *SPINNY* **ICK**Y *SHOWDOWN* Legal Department has a very important announcement about how to proceed!

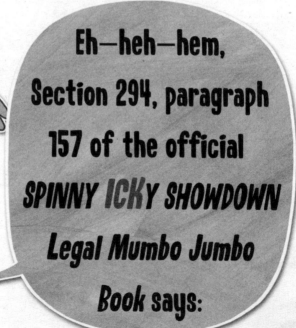

Eh—heh—hem, Section 294, paragraph 157 of the official *SPINNY* **ICK**Y *SHOWDOWN* *Legal Mumbo Jumbo* *Book* says:

# Under no circumstances

shall the wheel be spun more than ONCE per round. Therefore, if ANYTHING should disrupt a round of play, such as blood-thirsty tiCKs, then by default the category for that round shall be *SEASICK VOMIT LICK*!

Ewwww, that's even **MORE DISGUSTING!** Can we get the TICKs back?

GROSS!

Excuse me, Mr. Maverick, I think we can help. Carl Caveman and I fell in love during ROUND ONE and he just asked me to be his bride!

Me love her.

We want to get married and go on our honeymoon right away, so there's no need to eliminate any ICKSTERS in this round since we'll be leaving! Will you do the honors?

What do you say, Legal Department?

Eehhh, what the heck!

Then, BY ALL MEANS! Heeza Schmelly, do you take this *ICKSTER* to be your husband?

I DO!

And Carl Caveman, do you take this *ICKSTER* to be your wife??

Me DO!

# CHAPTER 9

After the newlyweds left, Leeza Schmelly and Baa-Baa both needed new teammates, and Leeza said Baa-Baa's curly fur makes him the perfect *CURLY-CUE*, so we're ready to go for **ROUND THREE!**

Ricky Maverick spun the wheel and it just passed NICK PUMPERNICKEL! Instead, it's going to land on . . .

**YOU PiCK the iCK!***

# WOOHOO!!!!!

This is the category everyone hopes for!

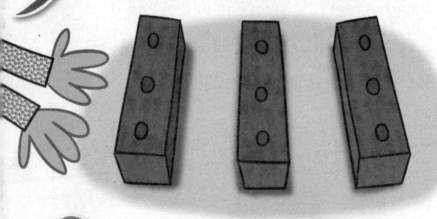

Listen up, *ICKSTERS*—whichever team picks the brick with the sticker on the other side gets to pick the *ICK* category!

That one!

That one!

Baa-baa!

Okay, this is a **REALLY BiG** decision that could **MAKE** or **BREAK** our chances of winning. I've watched **EVERY** episode of *The SPINNY ICKY SHOWDOWN* and the *ICKSTER* team that gets to *PICK the ICK* always chooses something that they think they'll be **GOOD** at.

There's **ANOTHER** option, though, that nobody **EVER** uses, and I think it could really help Peezo—and all of us for that matter. The only problem is that I know Peezo would **NEVER** agree to it!

*DOUGH BROS*, I need your *YOU PICK THE ICK* category, please.

I don't care which category, Arnie, as long as it's not—

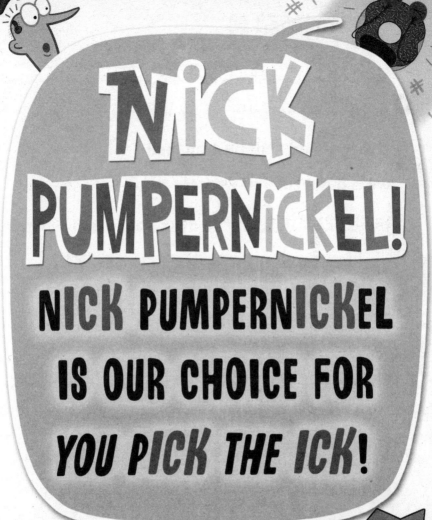

NICK PUMPERNICKEL!

NICK PUMPERNICKEL IS OUR CHOICE FOR *YOU PICK THE ICK*!

WHAT?!

I feel **AWFUL** springing that on Peezo the way I did, but I **HAD** to do it. If I hadn't, there would still be a chance we'd have to arm wrestle NICK PUMPERNICKEL in the next round and I just couldn't do that to Peezo. But with *THIS* strategy there's a **MYSTERY** ICK category under the *YOU PICK THE ICK* slot on the wheel that's only used if someone actually *CHOOSES* NICK PUMPERNICKEL for the *YOU PICK THE ICK* challenge. And whatever it is, NICK PUMPERNICKEL has to do it even if he's no good at it.

Little baby doughnut— the *PUMPERNATOR* is good at EVERYTHING!

But the **BEST THING** is that Peezo wouldn't have to worry about him **ANY-MORE**. Once everyone has challenged the *PUMPERNATOR* on the *YOU PICK THE ICK* round, his **NICK PUMPERNICKEL** category would be **REMOVED** from the wheel and replaced with a new category.

# VOILÀ!

## NO MORE NICK PUMPERNICKEL!

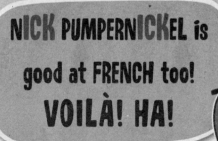

Pardonnez-moi, but *VOILÀ* is a French word pronounced *vwah-LA*. It means, "there you go" or, how you say,

NICK PUMPERNICKEL is good at FRENCH too! VOILÀ! HA!

All right, everyone, are you ready to see the category for the **YOU PICK THE ICK** challenge?

The Pumpernator will take you **ALL** down whatever the sissy category is!

HA! HA!

It looks like Nick Pumpernickel is ready. What about YOU, ICKSTERS?

READY!

READY!

READY!

BAA!

Not quite, but go ahead and reveal the challenge, Mr. Maverick.

Arnie's napkin

# CHAPTER 10

Here we go, *ICKSTERS*! The never-before-seen category under the *YOU PICK THE ICK* slot IS . . .

It's a little R U S T Y!

CREEeak!

GRUNT!

Errrr!

Got it!

PESKY PICKLE POGO STICK

Okay, **ICKSTERS**, with *PESKY PICKLE POGO STICK* you'll be POGO-ing with your plucky partner through *PICKLE PASS*, trying not to get pushed over by the *PERILOUS PIVOTING PEPPERED PICKLES* or pummeled by the *POWERFUL PEEWEE PICKLE PUNTER* or plunged into a *PESKY PICKLE JUICE PUDDLE!* WOW, that was a lot of **P**s!

That reminds me. I need to

You'll have to hold it, dear.

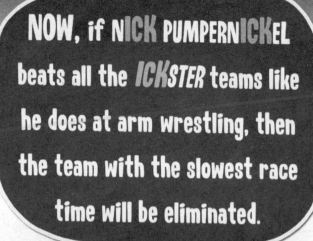

NOW, if N**ICK** PUMPERN**ICK**EL beats all the *ICKSTER* teams like he does at arm wrestling, then the team with the slowest race time will be eliminated.

If there's a TIE, we'll do a tie-breaker. BUT if by some MIRACLE any or ALL of you BEAT N**ICK** PUMPERN**ICK**EL, then you'll automatically go to the final round!

Take your pogo places, *ICKSTERS*!

Nick Pumpernickel is the *POGO-NATOR*!

Are you ready, Grandma?

You get on first.

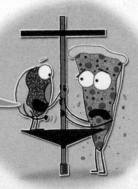

Come on, Peezo, you can DO this. You love the pogo stick!

THIS IS A SPINNY ICKY SHOWDOWN FIRST! EVERYONE BEAT NICK PUMPERNICKEL AND WILL MOVE TO THE FINAL ROUND! CONGRATULATIONS, ICKSTERS!
NO FAIR,
THE PUMPERNATOR GOT PICKLE JUICE IN HIS EYE AND COULDN'T SEE WHERE HE WAS GOING!
STUPID BUMPS AND LUMPS AND CLUMPS MADE THE PUMPERNATOR FALL!

WE! BEAT! NICK! Pumpernickel! WE! BEAT! NICK! PUMPERNICKEL!

97

# CHAPTER 11

Well, it looks like my strategy PAID OFF! Peezo is **SO HAPPY** now that he doesn't have to worry about NICK PUMPERNICKEL anymore! **FINALLY,** we can just have **FUN** and focus on winning the competition. GO, *DOUGH BROS!*

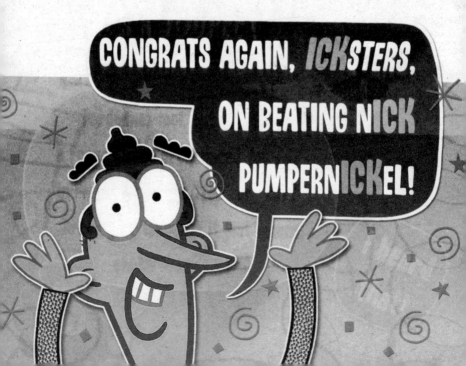

CONGRATS AGAIN, *ICK*STERS, ON BEATING NICK PUMPERN*ICK*EL!

There's **ONE** last challenge and here it is: RICKETY TOOTHPICK TIGHTROPE! For the final round of *THE SPINNY ICKY SHOWDOWN* you'll each be crossing a tightrope made only of toothpicks!

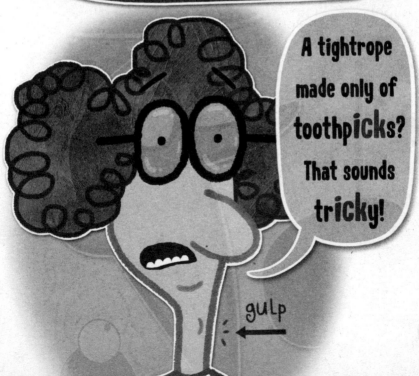

A tightrope made only of **toothpicks?** That sounds **tricky!**

gulp

**YES**, and it's even TRICKIER **kicking** your way across! To find our champions we'll combine both teammates' crossing times and **KICKS** together. The team with the fastest times and most **KICKS** will be the *SPINNY ICKY SHOWDOWN* **CHAMPIONS!**

But what if we fall off?

# GOOD QUESTION, LITTLE *ICKSTER!*

If you fall off, don't worry—you'll land in the soft pool of

## ICKY-STICKY-THICKY GOO!

Try to make it over to the tightrope ladder and get back in the race, but the

## ICKY-STICKY-THICKY GOO

is ICKY and stICKy **And THICKY!** so it's very hard to move around in! Are you ready to give it a go, *ICKSTERS?*

Even though I've never crossed a tight-rope before, I don't feel **SCARED**. Once, my neighbor **LoRetta Schmoretta's** cat was stuck up in a tree, and I walked across her balcony and clothesline to get him.

**Meow!**

I DIDN'T FALL OFF ONCE!

And Peezo is floating on air now that he's done worrying about NICK PUMPERNICKEL so he doesn't care HOW high up we'll be!

**BAWK BAAWWK**

Oooh, we're about ready to start!

**BAGAAAUUUK!**

And you're OFF, ICKSTERS!
Do we have to do this?
Be careful, Little G!

Peezo is so relaxed now that the *Pumpernator* is out of the picture that he's doing some really **IMPRESSIVE** kicks!

Big G is doing some great kicks too, and Little G is zipping right along, but poor Leeza Schmelly is so afraid of heights that she's clinging to Baa-Baa for dear life!

Way to go, Grandma G!

Hey, Peezo, just a little farther and— OUCH! Something just HIT me!

Me too!

LOOK! NICK PUMPERNICKEL is hiding behind that big clump of lumpy bumps! He's using the CHICKPEA SPITTER from another category to try to knock us down!

105

# THIS IS HORRIBLE!

Nick Pumpernickel is being such a **SORE LOSER!** We won **FAIR** and **SQUARE,** and now he doesn't want any of us to win!

# OH NO!

Nick Pumpernickel just knocked Little G off the tightrope into the Icky-Sticky-Thicky Goo!

Peezo, I'll be right back! Don't be afraid of Nick Pumpernickel and try not to let him knock you down!

Don't worry, Little G, I'll help you!

HELP!

Eeerrrr Ugghhhrrr Rrrrrr

Oh no! Now I'm stuck too!

110

It's not too late. We can both get back in the race, Little G!

Thanks, Arnie!

I'm back, Peezo!

Peezo—where ARE you?

PEEZO, WHAT ARE you DOING?!

# I CAN'T BELIEVE IT!

PEEZO IS CHASING NICK PUMPERNICKEL! Big G just told me that when Nick Pumpernickel knocked Little G off the tightrope, Peezo "BUSTED A CRUST" and jumped down and ran after him. OH NO! He's headed right for the *Grump on a Stump*'s yard!

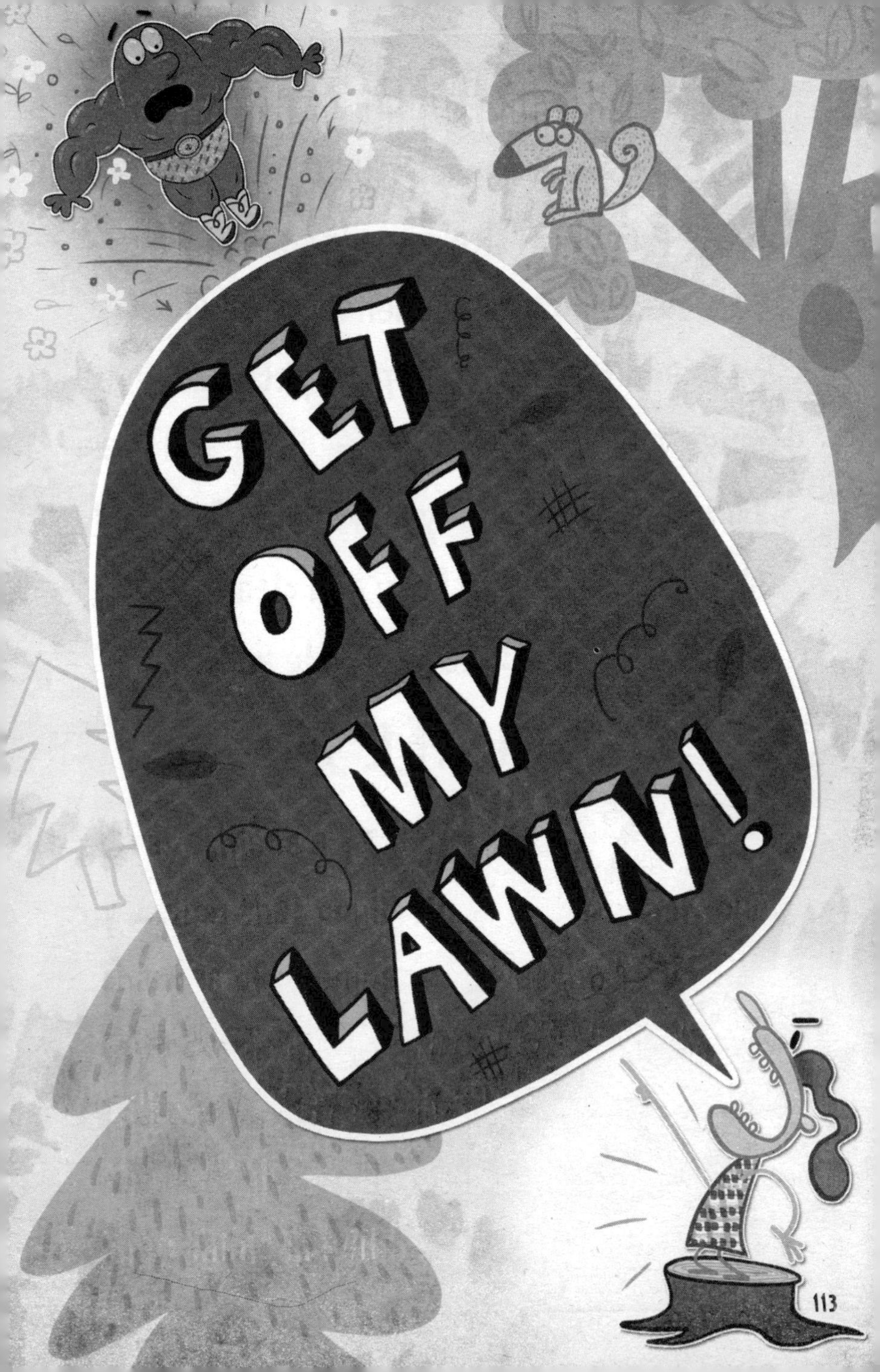
GET OFF MY LAWN!

# HOLEY DOUGHNUTS!

Peezo stopped himself JUST IN TIME but Nick Pumpernickel wasn't so lucky. He barreled into Maude Ellen Murky's flower beds and trampled her poor petunias! I've never seen her **SO mad** and the *Pumpernator* actually looks scared of her! She told him to get busy and clean up the GIANT MESS he made and he's

ACTUALLY

DOING

IT!

**AND THAT'S NOT ALL.** Keeping him company is the runaway P. P. Boy himself, Pikyor Pocketo! After he ran off with all the *nickels* from the *Chopstick Nickel Pick*, he tried taking a shortcut through the *Grump on a Stump*'s backyard.

# BiG MiSTAKE!

He plowed right through her vegetable garden and ruined her rutabagas!

I must say, it's pretty impressive to see how Maude Ellen Murky is handling it all. She could sure teach the *Law Lads* a thing or two

He went THIS way, I bet!

about catching criminals! She even got Pikyor Pocketo to give back the stolen nickels AND Ricky Maverick's wallet, watch, and toupee.

My WIG! I mean, TOUPEE!

# GOOD JOB, MAUDE ELLEN MURKY!

# CHAPTER 13

LET'S HEAR IT FOR THE LUMPY VALLEY SPINNY ICKY SHOWDOWN DOUBLE CHAMPIONS, THE GRAND GALS AND THE CURLY-CUES! CONGRATULATIONS!

Our name, Grandma!

Well, if the DOUGH BROS couldn't win THE SPINNY ICKY SHOWDOWN, I'm glad the *Grand Gals* did—and the *Curly-Cues* too. After the combination of

| | |
|---|---|
| Little G falling off the tightrope, | 😦 |
| Big G's fancy kicks, | 😊 |
| Leeza Schmelly's fear of heights, | 😦 |
| and Baa-Baa's calm, steady pace, | 😊 |

both teams ended up with the **EXACT SAME SCORE!** As for Peezo and me—things didn't really turn out like we had hoped, but that's okay.

Mr. Bing always says:

IT'S NOT WHETHER YOU WIN OR LOSE, IT'S HOW YOU PLAY THE GAME.

Or maybe it was:

THE WAY YOU PLAY DOESN'T MATTER BUT WINNING DOES SO DON'T LOSE!

NO, WAIT, I think it was—oh, I don't know.

BUT IT SURE WAS FUN!

AND, an unexpected **BONUS** of being on the show is that Peezo finally got over his fear of **NICK PUMPERNICK**EL. It was so brave of Peezo to run after him. And it looks like I'm not the only one who thinks so!

The only **BAD** thing about not winning is that I didn't get the new trophy friend for Stiffy Stu McShiny. I hope he won't be too disappointed.

Here, Arnie. I want you to have this.

Your propeller-spinning-penguin hat? *WHY?*

You could have won the *SPINNY ICKY SHOWDOWN* but you stopped to help me instead. It's my way of saying **THANK YOU.**

# THE END